Fluent Reader titles are ideal for children who can confidently read books with a wider vocabulary, and who are beginning to read longer stories by themselves.

Special features:

Full, exciting story

Richer, more

Suddenly, the class were by the castle walls from the book. They saw the turrets and the battlements. As they crossed over the moat, there was a huge splash.

"I wonder what that splash was," said Miss Zebra.

10

11

Detailed illustrations capture the imagination

Longer sentences

Clear type

But the lord of the castle, Lord Robert Fox, was looking very cross.

"My squire needs to help me get ready, but he's not here. I have trained a lot for the tournament, but I can't fight if I don't have my armour!"

"We'll help you to find your squire," Olivia said.

16

17

Ladybird

Educational Consultant: James Clements
Book Banding Consultant: Kate Ruttle
Subject Consultant: Philip Parker

LADYBIRD BOOKS

UK | USA | Canada | Ireland | Australia
India | New Zealand | South Africa

Ladybird Books is part of the Penguin Random House group of companies whose addresses can be found at global.penguinrandomhouse.com.

www.penguin.co.uk www.puffin.co.uk www.ladybird.co.uk

Penguin Random House UK

First published 2025
001

Written by Amy McCaw
Story by Ellen Philpott

Illustrations by Daniel Limon

With thanks to Child Autism UK and Pace

Printed in Dubai

The authorized representative in the EEA is Penguin Random House Ireland, Morrison Chambers, 32 Nassau Street, Dublin D02 YH68

A CIP catalogue record for this book is available from the British Library

ISBN: 978-0-241-67283-9

All correspondence to:
Ladybird Books
Penguin Random House Children's
One Embassy Gardens, 8 Viaduct Gardens, London SW11 7BW

Read It Yourself

Medieval Knights

Miss Zebra showed the class a huge history book.
"We're going to find out all about medieval castles!" she said.

Zara Penguin looked very excited.
"I love history!" she said.

"I love history, too," said Olivia Crocodile.

Miss Zebra opened the book. She showed the class the castle walls and the moat around them. Then, she showed them the turrets and battlements.

"I wonder what it was like in a medieval castle," said Olivia.

Suddenly, the class were by the castle walls from the book. They saw the turrets and the battlements. As they crossed over the moat, there was a huge splash.

"I wonder what that splash was," said Miss Zebra.

Everyone but Zara and Olivia followed Miss Zebra into the busy castle courtyard.

Suddenly, Zara heard someone crying.

"Can you hear crying?" she asked Olivia.

"I can hear it, too," said Olivia. They looked around, but they could not see where the sound was coming from.

In the courtyard, there were a lot of knights putting on their armour, with help from their squires.

More knights were training with pretend swords.

“This is where we train to fight,” a knight said. “You can pretend to fight, too.”

The class pretended to fight with swords. It was brilliant!

But the lord of the castle, Lord Robert Fox, was looking very cross.

"My squire needs to help me get ready, but he's not here. I have trained a lot for the tournament, but I can't fight if I don't have my armour!"

"We'll help you to find your squire," Olivia said.

“Thank you!” Lord Robert Fox said. “How are you going to do that?”

“We’ll go and look around the castle together,” said Zara.

“Very good,” said Lord Robert, “but you must go now, please! The king and queen are coming soon.”

In the huge castle kitchens, everyone was busy getting the delicious banquet food ready. Lady Isabel Fox was in the kitchen, too.

"No squires in here!" said Zara.

Zara and Olivia went back out through the courtyard. Again, they heard someone crying.

“Where is that crying coming from?” asked Zara.

“Over there,” said Olivia.

They followed the sound of crying.

"Don't cry!" called Zara. "If you come up here we can help you."

Up came Lord Robert's squire, Edward Deer.

"Please help me," Edward said. "I was bringing Lord Robert's armour into the castle, but I fell over. The armour fell into the moat. All I have now is this shield."

"We will help you find the armour," Olivia said.

“I can’t see the armour in all the reeds!” Edward Deer said. “Lord Robert is going to be so cross about this. What will I do?”

“The armour could be tangled in the reeds, so we can’t see it,” said Zara.

Suddenly, Zara said, “Look! I can see it! It’s tangled in the reeds over there!”

Now, they needed to free the heavy armour from the reeds.

"I wonder how we can get to it," said Olivia. "Could we swim to it?"

"I know! We can pull the armour out with the shield," Zara said.

"We must hold the shield together, Edward," said Olivia. "It's heavy!"

"I can get the armour back!" said Edward Deer.

Suddenly, there was a splash.

“Please help me!” said Edward Deer. “I can’t swim!”

"Hold on to the shield!" said Zara.

"And bring the armour with you!" said Olivia.

Edward got the shield and freed the armour.

Then, Olivia pulled the squire and the armour out of the moat.

"Thank you for your help!" said the squire.

The class and Edward Deer went to Lord Robert. He was very happy to see Edward and the armour.

"Thank you, all," Lord Robert said. "Would you like to come to the banquet after the tournament?"

"We would!" said Miss Zebra.

Then, it was time for the tournament. Knights in armour pretended to fight with swords. It was very exciting!

After the tournament, everyone went to the banquet. The food was delicious! The king and queen then thanked Lord Robert and Lady Isabel for the tournament.

“You must thank Zara Penguin and Olivia Crocodile, too!” said Lord Robert.

"Medieval castles are brilliant!" Zara said.

"The tournament was very good – and I loved the food!" Olivia said.

How much do you remember about the story of *Medieval Knights*? Answer these questions and find out!

- What parts of a castle does Miss Zebra show to the class?
- What can Zara Penguin and Olivia Crocodile hear someone doing?
- What do all the knights put on?
- Who helps them?
- Why is Edward Deer upset?
- How do Olivia and Zara help Edward Deer?
- What does Lord Robert Fox invite the class to?